# Gone in a flash

## PAT SIMMONS

Gone in a Flash
ISBN 978-1-76109-705-8
Copyright © text Pat Simmons 2025
Cover Design: Graham Davidson

First published 2025 by
**Ginninderra Press**
PO Box 2 Bentleigh 3204
ginninderrapress.com.au

# Contents

# Going Home

I'm back from a year overseas. Mum's in a retirement home.

She's written many times saying how lovely it is.

It isn't.

The room is tiny, the shabby carpet a dreadful aubergine colour.

The room smells.

I notice Mum tense, her hand on her tummy.

'Dystopia,' she says.

I grin.

'I think you mean dyspepsia, Mum. Dystopia's a sort of undesirable, frightening, environmentally degraded world.'

Silence.

'Mum, remember the first place I rented? You came to visit and dragged me home?'

She nods, smiling.

'My turn now, and you got the word right the first time.'

I start packing her bags.

# Breaking News

Global Corporation Nursery Rhyme Inc. has announced the dismissal of three key executives.

Ms M. Hubbard, whose cupboards are continually bare, sacked from her position as Chief Dog Minder.

Mr G. Porgie, who kissed girls and made them cry, charged with inappropriate sexual behaviour.

Ms B. Peep denied that she abandoned sheep, insisting that if she left them alone, they would come home. The sheep are in the care of an animal rescue organisation.

Investigations continue regarding an unnamed farmer's wife accused of severing the tails of three mice with a carving knife.

Further sackings are expected to be announced.

# Homeless

She strokes the bright red patch of velvet, soft to the touch, protected for decades by the embroidered antimacassar.

The rest of the sofa is faded, tired. Just like she is. The china cabinet, bereft of its contents, glass doors cracked, wobbles uncertainly, threatening to fall.

Her grandmother was her best friend, her protector. We all need a best friend, don't we?

People pull up, stare. Some poke at the sofa, sort through the cardboard box of odds and ends.

'Can I take this china?'

She nods.

Back at the hostel she fingers the embroidery.

It's all she has left.

# Just Another Wednesday

The regime at the Sunshine Nursing Home is probably necessary, but incredibly boring.

Today's Wednesday.

Walkers, wheelchairs and walking sticks board the minibus.

The residents are off to the local shopping centre.

This Wednesday is the same as any other, at least as far as the staff are concerned.

The driver parks at the shopping centre. He and the carers disembark.

Before they have a chance to set up the ramp, Sprightly Jack Higgins, the leader of the conspiracy, hops into the driver's seat and starts the engine.

'Where to, ladies and gents?'

'As far away as possible,' they chorus.

# Decision Time

'She's horrible, isn't she?'

His sister agreed. 'Lots of people are horrible.'

'True,' he murmured.

'They don't get punished.'

'It's a dilemma all right.' He shook his head.

They sat, chewing on liquorice sticks, wondering what to do next.

Eyes streaming, they considered their position.

They were out of their depth. This was grown-up stuff. Never having had to make a decision like this before, they'd acted on the spur of the moment.

They could've just legged it.

Simultaneously, they grabbed the old woman and put the hose on her.

There's nothing worse than the aroma of smoking witch.

# Healthy Choices

Suzie's a good friend but she can be a little superior.

We meet for breakfast.

'Bacon and eggs?' I suggest.

She gives me THE look.

'Sweetie you know I never eat anything with a face. Muesli with raspberry yogurt please.'

I'm munching away, she's picking, when I actually remember a fact from a drunken Trivial Pursuit game.

'Beetles have faces,' I comment.

'Raspberry yogurt,' I add smugly.

Suzie pauses mid-spoonful.

'Red cochineal beetles. They dry them, crush them and make a red dye called carmine. It's in some yogurts.'

'Bugger it!' she sighs and grabs a slice of my bacon.

# Home Invasion

The family was distressed and confused.

The child whimpered.

Why would someone do this to their little home? They lived simply and had little in the way of possessions.

Why them?

The policeman shook his head sadly. So much destruction and yet the family confirmed that nothing had been stolen.

Smashed crockery and broken furniture littered the modest little home.

The policeman stooped to meet the eyes of the perpetrator.

'Don't you realise that if you'd chosen the smallest bowl, the smallest chair and the smallest bed, you wouldn't be in so much trouble.

Goldilocks hung her head in shame.

# Panic

In one week. Just one week. That's when it's happening.

I should never have decided to do it. It's too late to turn back now.

As the day draws nearer, my panic attacks increase. I'm terrified. I've planned it as best I can but this will be a first for me. Something I never thought I would attempt.

I realise that others have survived, but will I?

Well, this is it. The day has arrived. I feel numb. I can't stop trembling.

Twelve six-year-old boys are arriving at my small apartment to help my son celebrate his birthday.

# Lost Words

She shuffles into the library, odd shoes, shabby wet raincoat, walking stick.

The library staff greet her kindly.

'She'll either be reading The Tempest because it's pouring out there, or that poetry book she carries around,' one whispers.

It's the poetry book. Spectacles perched on her nose, she reads out loud in her quavering voice.

A curious child approaches her, despite the mother's warning hiss.

The child is enchanted, as is the mother, who moves closer.

She closes the book but continues to recite the poem.

The mother picks up the book, studying the photograph.

'You wrote this?'

She nods.

# Precious

He finally has the key, the precious key. He never thought the day would come when he would be trusted with the key. He feels empowered.

He wonders how to keep it safe. Carefully, lovingly, he threads it onto a piece of string and ties the string around his neck. He tucks it into his shirt. No one will see it and try to take it from him.

Later that day, he proudly, tentatively, unlocks the door.

Parked in the next street, his mother breathes a sigh of relief. Her son is home from school safely and didn't lose the key.

# The Garden

He rakes the sand, creating ripples.

He moves rocks to new positions. This takes time. He gives much thought to the placement of the rocks.

His garden is his solace, helping him to relax and control his anger.

Life has been unkind. So much has gone wrong. Was it his fault? He doesn't think so.

He's proud of his creation. A tobacco tin filled with sand, stones he found lying around the yard, a statue he made in pottery class and the rake, fashioned from an old toothbrush.

His own Zen garden in his prison cell. It's there for life.

# The Report

Tentatively she hands him the report. He smiles, then frowns.

'George prefers to engage in parallel play and tends not to socialise with his peers. On occasions, he does not listen to instructions and ignores his teachers. George can be a little stubborn and will sometimes refuse to take part in physical exercise, preferring to sit quietly and watch others. He has some difficulty sharing, but this may improve as he matures. He can, on occasions, be a little disruptive.'

'Come on, love,' she says soothingly, 'don't be too hard on him. It's only his third week at puppy school.'

# Trapped

He's panicking. He begins to perspire. Lost, confused, afraid, he wonders how he can escape.

With trembling hands, he clings to his mobile and rings her.

No response, so he texts.

How could you do this to me? How could you send me to such a diabolical place? I'm overwhelmed. I don't know which way to turn. Get me out of here.

He waits, eyes darting, hoping that alcohol is available somewhere.

His phone rings.

For heaven's sake Tom, get a grip. All I asked you to do was pop into Ikea and pick up those bookshelves we need.

# Woops!

I'm no superhero. I'm not brave or anything like that, but I hate seeing anyone being bullied or physically hurt in any way.

I'm walking home from work. It's getting dark and I hear a woman screaming.

Then I see her. A man has hold of her and is shouting obscenities at her. She's crying, trying to pull away from him.

He raises his hand to hit her. I can't stand it and spring into action, lunging at the man.

'Oh, for heaven's sake, get that idiot off the set.'

Then I notice the cameras.

'Take two,' sighs someone.

# Family

At the polished antique dining table, the solicitor organises his paperwork. He surveys the family.

He reads, 'To my daughter, Dorothea, I leave my jewellery and my collection of first edition books.'

Silence.

'To my granddaughter, Felicity, I leave $1,000.00 and my teddy bear collection.'

Granddaughter squeaks with delight.

'To my son, Sebastian, I leave my furniture and motor cars.'

Silence.

'My house and other real estate acquisitions will be sold and the proceeds donated to the Sunshine Home, where Bianca will reside for the remainder of her life.'

Outrage.

The majestic Bianca, purring contentedly, jumps onto the solicitor's lap.

# Black Knight

'What would I do without you, Jim? You're my knight in shining armour. Cup of tea, dear?'

'Yes please, Mrs Pemberton.'

Jim's just mowed her lawn, read her the little booklet she received about home care and fixed the flyscreen door.

He's also found fifty dollars in cash and some old coins which he's pocketed.

His handyman business is going well. Pick the oldies. They're the ones with the treasures.

Satisfied, Mrs P. removes her mobile phone from her walker and makes the call.

'Out like a light, officer. No hurry, dear. I popped a little something in his tea.'

# Horror

I'm trapped, with little likelihood of escape. Trapped, like a flimsy paperback between two heavy bookends. I'm not frightened, just tired and a little overwhelmed.

What will happen if I try to escape? If only I could reach my phone but I can't move my arms.

I'm hot and sweaty and judging from the aromas surrounding me, so are they. I shouldn't be in this situation. It's my own fault.

Oh, thank goodness, one of them is moving away, others are scrambling through the doors.

At last I can sit down. Never again will I catch a peak hour train.

# Permission Granted

It was a noisy day in parliament, with hoots of derision and a great deal of heckling. But staunch left-winger, Ms Blinker, was determined to support her colleague.

Life choices had nothing to do with fellow parliamentarians, as long as the honourable member resumed duties when parliament sat again. Ms Blinker demanded open-mindedness and the full support of the house.

Feathers were ruffled but it was agreed that the request for special leave be granted.

Should an owl and a pussycat choose to go to sea and subsequently be married, they were quite within their rights to do so.

# The Reunion

The night is young and the members congregate. Despite having experienced centuries of bigotry, they remain comrades and gourmets, albeit in a rather unusual area of cuisine.

Group A members admit that their food choice is a little bland but point out that their diet supports longevity.

Group B challenges Group A, insisting that their choice of diet is so much tastier and sustains them even longer than Group A members.

Group O, far more positive, insist that their diet sustains them for hundreds of years and is definitely not bland.

The Vampire View Club raise their glasses of red.

# Beltane

My stinging eyes are watering and ash is clinging to my sweaty skin as we move between the flames.

I reckon my grandfather would've been proud of me.

I loved listening to stories about my Irish ancestors when I was a kid – wonderful stories.

Such a rich culture.

At this moment in time I'm reminded of the Beltane Festival Dad used to tell us about; the bonfires, the feasting and how they believed that the smoke and ashes had protective powers.

But this isn't a Beltane Festival. This is an Australian bushfire. The animals are terrified and so am I.

# The Mission

The cat is sleek. The cat is stealthy. The cat is on a mission.

She understands that the task will not be easy but the satisfaction from its accomplishment will be huge.

She excels at jumping onto furniture, fences or anything she considers interesting.

She enjoys the challenge.

Leaping onto the pile of bricks, she bats with left paw, then her right.

Exhausted, she rests before trying again.

There's a long pause while she wills herself to complete the mission.

Finally the egg falls to the ground and smashes.

A catastrophe indeed.

Such is the untold story of Humpty Dumpty.

# Our Mum

Clearing Mum's house is upsetting.

The Eiffel Tower ashtray is tossed into the bin along with the bullfighter tea towel.

A string of bunting from a street carnival goodness knows where.

Tiny clogs. 'Can I have these?' my sister asks.

'Sure,' I say, 'as long as you take the musical windmill too.'

'No way!'

The sails turn, each one flashing a different coloured light. It plays 'Tulips from Amsterdam.'

We're laughing and crying. The wine's probably to blame.

'How long has she got?' I ask my sister.

'Five years this time. Told her she was too old for drug smuggling.'

# The Wake-up Call

I've lost count of how many years we've been together. They've blurred into a living hell.

My life's a nightmare. I can do nothing right. She's never satisfied.

The house is too small. We don't have enough servants.

I live in abject misery.

Trouble is, she has this fairy tale idea of how her life should be. I keep telling her she's living in the past.

It's my own fault. I made a monumental error, with the emphasis on 'mental'.

I should've ridden straight past the castle and some other sucker would've woken her up from her hundred-year sleep.

# Hope

Grandad was a stonemason. He was a craftsman, my dad used to say.

Dad was a brickie. He'd take me to work with him. He'd give me a little trowel and I'd 'help' him. He was a tradesman.

They've both gone. Long gone.

Me? I was factory fodder.

I built a wall but it wasn't made from bricks or stones.

It was an imagined wall. A wall of doubt. A wall of loss. A wall to keep people out.

Until one day, a voice in my head said, 'Be a sculptor.'

My inner wall crumbles as I caress the stone.

# The Perfect Female

He's nervous. He's never responded to an online ad before.

Is this the right thing to do?

Is she a victim of exploitation?

Most probably.

How old is she?

She's young, he's told. Would you like a picture? I'll send one.

He waits. The photo arrives. She looks beautiful, dark-haired, lithe and she has such kind eyes.

He's smitten. He wants her. 'What's the next step?' he asks, his fingers trembling on the key pad.

Come and meet her. This is the address.

He takes one look at her and he's in love.

This is his first greyhound rescue.

# Rite of Passage

He enters the room, walking with that exaggerated swagger some young men adopt when they're trying to look tough.

We exchange looks. I can see he's scared.

'Is this your first time?' I ask him.

'Yeah.'

'Take your shirt off and lie down.'

He fumbles with the shirt buttons, his hands trembling.

He obviously works out. 'Great torso,' I comment.

He blushes.

'Would you like to look at some pictures?' I ask.

'I know what I want but it's gonna hurt, isn't it? His eyes fixed on mine.

'A bit, maybe, but don't worry, I'm the best female tattooist around.'

# Washed Out

He's an artist, a poet, a sensitive talented man. Each picture belongs with a poem. Each poem clings to its picture.

Head down, frowning, concentrating on his work. It's a cloudy day. Clouds are inspiring. Clouds create poetry.

He grins and mutters to himself, 'I wandered lonely as a cloud…still wandering.'

The first raindrops begin to dilute his work. The chalk runs. The colours blur.

Pictures and poetry are drowning.

Down the drain they flow. A day's creations underground.

He picks up the few coins, sips from the bottle in its brown paper jacket and limps back to the hostel.

# The Uninvited Guest

I froze. The body was just…lying there. I stared from one face to the other, but they didn't care.

How could they be so heartless?

Some of them were actually smiling.

My nightmare continued. Disposal of the body was beyond me. I began to feel physically sick. I was afraid I might faint.

I had to do something. I couldn't appear weak in front of the others. I took deep breaths and pulled myself together.

I tried not to look at the dreadful thing, the foreign body.

I raised my hand. 'Waiter,' I screeched, 'there's a fly in my soup.'

# The Deal

My nerves are in tatters. This is such torture.

What am I to do? It's my own fault. I'm so weak.

I allowed this to happen, aware of the possible consequences. I'd been warned but had assured everyone that it was fine. What a fool I've been.

Perhaps I could bargain with him. I approach his room. Hesitantly, I push open the door. He doesn't hear me.

The noise is unbearable.

With lightning speed, I disarm him.

He cries out.

'If you let me throw this bloody recorder in the bin, I'll buy you a guitar,' I say.

He grins. 'Deal.'

# A New Day

Joe walks through the gates. Sunshine mixed with rain creates a rainbow. He gazes at the sky and grins. A new day. A new life.

The thought of this new life both exhilarates and scares him. His daily routine kept him safe. Now there may be chaos.

He thinks about his mates. Will he see them again? He figures he probably will.

Some would say that Joe's paid his debt to society. But Joe doesn't see it quite like that.

Because Joe wasn't guilty of killing his wife.

But he knows who was. And he knows where the bastard lives.

# Maybe, Maybe Not

'What's dementia?' I ask.

'It's when you're bad-tempered and can't remember anything,' Gran mutters.

'Is there a cure?' I ask.

'Of course not. Get in the car.'

When we arrive at the nursing home, Grandad's playing cards with an old lady. They're laughing.

Until they see us coming.

'It's no good talking to him,' Gran sniffs.

So we sit in silence. Grandad stares blankly at the television screen. So do we.

'Let's go.' Gran sighs and heads for the exit.

Grandad grabs my arm and whispers, 'Hi, Joe. How's my favourite grandson today?'

He grins and winks at me.

# The Accident

His grimace of pain did nothing to soften his mother's heart.

'What have I told you about running without shoes on,' she scolded.

He was too weak to retaliate. She was right after all. He gazed ruefully at his heavily bandaged foot.

After so much feasting and dancing, he'd kicked off his shoes at the end of the evening. It had been such a wonderful night.

He sighed, then frowned. He called for his servant.

'As soon as I can walk again, we will scour the land and find the complete idiot who left a glass slipper on the stairs.'

# Quiet Carriage

He sits in the 'Quiet Carriage' and opens his laptop. He regrets that he had a late night.

The report's due today. His boss is fussy. He taps at the keys.

He reads what he's written so far. All good.

Oh no! He fell asleep. The train's arrived at the city. He slaps the laptop shut and races from the station into his office.

He grabs a coffee, prints off the report and reads it through.

With the confidence of a young executive, he admires his prowess. Until he reads the last line.

'You look very attractive when you're asleep.'

# Routine

Every day's the same. She goes to the same place, at the same time, sits on the same seat, and waits.

It's a lonely routine but she's determined to turn things around.

She's tried other ways to earn a crust. This is her last hope.

The place has a hypnotic feel. The lights, the sounds, she's drawn to them. A false sense of security.

She ignores the warning signs they put up.

She's emptied the kids' money boxes today. She'll pay them back.

The rent's due and there's no food left.

The machine will pay up today. It has to.

# Stage-struck

She steps confidently onto the stage. Her long slender legs and graceful movements are mesmerising.

She takes her time. There is no hurry. This is what she's worked so hard to achieve and she's savouring every magical second of it. There have been so many setbacks, but her sheer genius and grim determination to succeed are finally paying off.

Nothing will get in her way now. She's unstoppable. She slowly, seductively approaches those who are watching.

Fascinated, eyes wide, they are a captive audience. Frozen in time, wondering what her next move will be.

She eats the succulent blowfly first.

# The Book

I squeeze into the packed train.

The woman next to me wants to chat.

I just want to finish my book. Political conspiracy, suspense, violence.

It's got the lot.

'Good book?' cheery woman asks.

I show her the cover

'I've seen the movie,' she chirps.

I avoid eye contact.

She turns to the guy on her other side, but he's wearing headphones.

I close the book. I'll finish it tonight, alone, in peace.

'You've finished it?'

'No.'

Cheery woman isn't a listener.

'Who would've thought Sarah was the spy and killed all those people.'

I want to kill cheery woman.

# Bloody Mary

I enjoy having coffee with Mary, though she is a bit of a 'know all'.

Yesterday, after our coffee, we browsed the op shops. I found a plate with a delightful floral design. I had plans for that plate.

Mary always looks for a 'treasure.' She watches far too many of those antique shows. She insisted on taking a photo of my plate, both sides.

She rang me this morning. Apparently, the plate is rare and is worth almost one thousand dollars.

I regard the hundreds of tiny plate pieces, smashed ready for my next mosaic class and swear profusely.

# An Annual Event

Armed with donations, Maggie's first stop is the nursing home. Chocolates for everyone.

Then the charity shop. An assortment of dreadful soaps which she suspects came from a discount warehouse.

Maggie detours to the animal shelter. Two crocheted blankets to keep the kittens warm.

She rummages through her bag. A feather boa. Now who did I mean to give that to? Oh yes.

The staff at the child care centre love it when Maggie visits. They add the boa and two large cotton nighties to the dress-up box.

Maggie smiles with satisfaction. Mission accomplished. Those dreadful Christmas presents successfully re-gifted.

# Old Friends

Dear Eileen,

Received the photograph you sent. Personally, I find those large hotels rather common. Where is it, dear?

Jim's left me.

*Dear Marjorie,*

*Thank you for your email and photo of your cats. You may remember that I loathe cats.*

*Sorry about Jim.*

Dear Eileen,

You may prefer this photo of the Louvre. I don't believe you've ever been to France, have you dear?

No word from Jim.

*Dear Marjorie,*

*I would suggest you pay a visit to an Egyptian necropolis where treasured cats were buried with their owners.*

*Jim and I are holidaying in Paris at the moment.*

# A Fond Farewell

He gently takes her hand. 'I don't want to leave you. But I'm told I'm a loser.'

'I don't want you to go. Why must you go?' she sobs.

'My time is up.'

Hand in hand they gaze into space.

He turns to her, frowning and gently touches her eyelids. 'What is this moisture?'

She brushes away her tears. 'I'm crying. I'm crying because I'll miss you so much.'

'Crying? I don't know crying. Perhaps it's not in my program.'

'It's not Rob,' says the white-coated technician, 'which is why I must close you down and introduce the new model.'

# The Collection

Memories surround him. Each handbag tells a story. The year, the season, time, place, passion and loss.

The colourful cotton Balinese bag, the soft Italian leather clutch, the gold mesh evening purse, the finely embroidered Indian handbag. Each one a treasure.

The newest suede drawstring bag feels so soft, so sensuous. The contents are much the same as usual. Compact, lipstick, wallet, phone. They are of little importance.

He smiles as he views his treasures, each hanging on its own special hook.

His collection.

Lovingly he finds a place for his newest, youngest acquisition.

So many bags, So many murders.

# Betrayal

I'm tired, so tired, and ashamed of who I am.

I wander from place to place, seeking, I'm not sure what. Acceptance I suppose.

But it may be too late.

In the beginning my journey was exciting. Everything was new. There were many possibilities for someone like me.

I had the whole world at my fingertips.

I marvelled at the trees, the flowers, the clouds. All that nature had to offer.

Then rejection broke my heart.

I moved on and on. Rejection pursued me. I craved company. I demanded company.

But it was denied me.

Victor Frankenstein, you betrayed me.

# The Trainer

He's a motivational trainer. I'm sure he's good at his work. He's certainly got us trained. He only has to look at the dog and she's licking his boots.

Where is he now? Out bike riding, training for the big race. When's the race? On my birthday. Has he realised that? I doubt it.

Offensive, isn't it?

Even the garden's trained. He spends hours out there, clipping at the foliage.

Clipping wings – that's his talent.

The hedges are particularly well trained. Hedges create boundaries, walls, screens. He likes that.

He's a topiary terrorist.

But I'm out here, sharpening the secateurs.

# The Gathering

She hated parties. Pretending to like people you couldn't stand, worrying about what to wear. The list went on.

She hadn't received an invitation to this party. Why was she there?

She didn't want to be rude, but what a bunch of weirdos!

Even a stiff drink straight from the bottle wasn't going to improve this situation.

They were reciting poetry for goodness sake.

She moved around the table. So did the guy with the big hat and the fellow with the big ears.

The little guy was asleep. She didn't blame him.

'This is a bloody nightmare,' Alice muttered.

# Undignified

The first costume is ridiculous. I'm a ladybird. They smile condescendingly as they film.

Next, a tutu. Extremely scratchy.

Will the indignity ever end?

I'm consoled by the fact that I haven't left the house. Unlike previous photo shoots when I was dragged to a miscellany of locations I would never visit by choice.

'Last change of clothes, Sweetie,' someone simpers.

Where is Saint Gertrude of Nivelles* when you need her?

A leather jacket, bandana and sunglasses. I think not.

I display my lack of amusement by yowling, scratching and refusing those ghastly, so called, cat treats they offer me.

* Saint Gertrude – patron saint of cats

# Reckless

I've always been obsessed with towers. I suppose Freud would have something to say about that.

I love them; the Leaning Tower of Pisa, the Tower of London, The Eiffel Tower, even Centre Point Tower.

Then there are the wonderful stories where a tower is of great significance, Rapunzel for example.

I shouldn't have done it. It was foolish, reckless and dangerous. But for once I wanted to live on the edge.

So, grocery list in one hand, walking stick in the other, I shuffled into the supermarket, wielded my stick and knocked down the tower of baked bean cans.

# The Traveller

I sometimes catch the early train to the city.

I listen to the other passengers.

The things they talk about on their mobile phones!

My goodness!

But mostly I catch the 10 a.m. It takes me a while to walk to the station with my old legs.

I listen to the older people's conversations. They like to talk about medical appointments and what they ate on their cruises.

When I reach the city, I catch the train home again. To the telly and two-minute noodles.

That's my life.

On reflection, I wouldn't call myself an eavesdropper.

I just like listening.

# Making the best of it

I like that expression – surf the net. I'm quite an expert. Not that I've ever been in the surf, physically I mean. The internet is my best friend.

I've just done my grocery shopping online. Sometimes you get free samples with the delivery. I like that. Alcohol too, left at the door.

And books online. I love reading.

There's so much information on the internet. Use it to pay my bills.

I even look at those dating sites. What a hoot! Sometimes I'm tempted.

I haven't actually been outside my house for two years, but I'm all right, honestly.

# The Solution

They terrify me. I've tried to overcome my fear but I can't. I have nightmares about clusters of them, creeping onto my skin.

Wherever I go, they're there. At the gym, the sauna, the pool, everywhere.

Their webs, so intricate. Their colours, red, blue and black. What to do? This is destroying my life. I need to get a grip, get some help.

No need to take time off work and no need to stay in hospital?

No surgery necessary. But do I have the cash?

Yep – forget the holiday. This is more important.

A curse upon those spider veins.

# Expect the Unexpected

The sensation was strange and most uncomfortable. She realised that she should've been more aware, more knowledgeable, more careful about her choice of drink. But the damage had been done.

Sadly, she was too young to understand that her drink had probably been spiked.

She was alone. No one to blame. No one to help her.

She knew that she had to deal with the situation as best she could. The room was spinning. The furniture looked different, smaller somehow.

When the windows finally smashed to accommodate her giant body, Alice realised that it was going to be one of those days.

# Decision Time

The sensible decision is to make the move. Everyone says so. My friends, family, even the nice man at the coffee shop.

'It'll be perfect for you. Everything you need,' they croon in that patronising and rather dominant way humans speak to older humans who are over the age of seventy.

But will it?

I've studied the brochure, checked my bank balance and considered my options.

Relaxing with my gin and tonic, I tear the brochure for the Sunshine Retirement Home into tiny pieces and place the pieces in the sick bag in front of me.

Paris, here I come.

# Moving On

It takes guts to slam the door. No one will hear the gesture but it makes her feel good.

Why did she decide to help these guys out? They've been kind, but she needs to move on.

Yes, they took her in, but as a domestic? So disappointing.

Life's a journey, right? She helped them out. She tidied up their place, cooked for them, cleaned their boots, had a roof over her head.

But when spooky old women start knocking on the door asking her to taste apples, that's weird, yes?

Snow White decides to change her name to Ebony Black.

# Book Club

The once a month, Tuesday night meeting.

As usual, I'm late.

When I arrive, they're discussing sociopaths.

'Brilliant sociopath this month,' says Amy.

'More like a psychopath,' I mutter.

'Oh, I wouldn't call him a psychopath,' says Mary. 'He's rather cute in his Harris Tweed suit.'

'Oh, come on,' I exclaim, sipping my Shiraz. 'Never mind what he wears, he's a cannibal, for goodness sake.'

Triumphantly, I pull the book from my bag.

Silence of the Lambs.

'That was last month when you were away,' squeals Amy as she holds up The Wind in the Willows.

'Poor Toad,' we giggle.

# So Close

Standing at the roadside, savouring the darkness, the riskiness of it all, she shivers with excitement. Glad she missed the last bus, she can tell her friends that she hitched a lift. They'll freak out. She grins to herself.

A car approaches, music blaring, slowing down. Stopping.

'Hop in,' they shout.

She's sobering up.

A moment of silence before they drive off, yelling obscenities.

'We'll be back,' they jeer.

Legs like jelly, raw fear, as a second car roars down the westbound carriageway. Then stops.

The man looks angry but he has kind eyes.

'Get in the car.'

'Thanks, Dad.'

# The Experiment

She's frightened. Was this the right thing to do? It's too late now. She tries to relax.

How harmful will these chemicals be? Will they burn me? She's scared to ask those who have the answers.

The timer ticks away the minutes. Tension builds. Finally, the timer rings so loudly that she nearly jumps out of her skin.

She complies with their requests. The warm water calms her but the drying machine renews her fear.

'Why are your eyes closed?'

'I'm scared,' she replies.

'Open them.'

'I love it. I've always wanted to be a blonde.'

She hugs the hairdresser.

# Garage Sale

Furniture

Toys

Bikes

Tools

He sticks the Garage Sale sign out the front.

He picks up the rubbish, including the empty Coke bottle and Mentos wrapper. Reminders of when he made a volcano with his kids. They love experiments.

He's tried so hard. Just can't do anything right. He's been off the grog for a year. But he's lost his job. Last in, first out, as usual.

She said she understood. But he's angry at himself. Angry at the world.

She and the kids have left.

He stacks everything out the front. The house is empty.

Except for the shotgun.

# After the Fall

'He has concussion and a very nasty cut. What happened?' asks the doctor.

'I'm not sure. He just said he fell down.'

'Hmm,' says the doctor. 'I know you believe in these old-fashioned remedies but I must insist that he's taken to the hospital immediately.'

He glares with suspicion at the empty bucket, the paper bags and the blood spots on the floor.

'Oh no, doctor, he'll be fine, honestly. Besides, we must wait here for Jill.'

'Where is she?' asks the doctor.

The room stinks of vinegar.

'I'm not sure, doctor. Someone said that she came tumbling after.'

## About the Author

Pat lives at Scarborough on the south coast of New South Wales with her cats, Mr. Meowgi and Oscar.

Prior to devoting her time to writing, Pat worked in children's services for over 20 years, in Early Childhood, Out of School Hours Care, the National Maritime Museum as Kids' Deck Coordinator, and as a Tafe teacher.

Pat is a writer of poetry, short stories, flash fiction and children's picture books.

Her poetry has been published in children's literary magazines including *School Magazine* and has won awards in the UK and Australia.

www.patsimmonswriter.com.au